G

'Oh d   een
chuckl   ard
anythir   . so
much I

'Same here,' Tommy agreed from the floor. 'Mum was right. That ghost really is funny. I hope he comes back every night.'

As both children began to laugh again, George turned slowly and sadly away, two great ghost tears running down his cheeks. Now he knew the awful truth. He was a failure. He was the first ghost in the whole of history who made people laugh instead of terrifying them out of their wits.

GEORGE H. GHASTLY

Ritchie Perry

Illustrated by Chris Winn

Beaver Books

*This book is dedicated to my mother
and father as some small return for all the
help and encouragement they have given me.
It is also for Tina and Sara who kept asking
why I didn't write a book for them.*

A Beaver Book
Published by Arrow Books Limited
62–65 Chandos Place, London WC2N 4NW

An imprint of Century Hutchinson Limited

London Melbourne Sydney Auckland
Johannesburg and agencies throughout the world

First published by Hutchinson Children's Books 1981

Beaver edition 1987
Reprinted 1987

Text © Ritchie Perry 1981
Illustrations © Chris Winn 1987

Printed and bound in Great Britain by
Anchor Brendon Ltd, Tiptree, Essex

ISBN 0 09 952020 6

One

Everybody else said the cobweb sandwiches were out of this world, but George was far too excited to eat anything. The moment he had been waiting for came when Mr Wraith stepped up on to the stage, looking very smart in his best shroud. When he called for silence everybody immediately put down their plates and cups and turned to face him.

'Ghosts, ghouls and apparitions,' Mr Wraith began, speaking with the voice for which he was famous. It sounded rather like the rusty hinges of a cemetery gate at midnight. 'As you are all aware, I have only been headmaster of the Academy of Ghosts for two hundred and sixty years. Indeed, if it hadn't been for Mrs Lucifer's unfortunate accident with the exorcist I might not have become headmaster at all. However, even as a relative newcomer, I know Speech Day means as much to you as it does to the rest of the staff and myself. It is a proud moment for any parent when a child reaches its hundredth birthday and is about to venture forth on the great adventure of death.

'I realize that many of you do not completely understand the new teaching methods. Some of you may even disapprove of them. Nevertheless, I can promise you that those pupils who are receiving their Certificates of Haunting today are as well schooled as any who have left the Academy before them. All of them have a thorough understanding of the three Ss, as was shown by the end of term exams and in their special studies. . . .'

Mr Wraith went on and on and on. With only one Speech Day every hundred years, he wasn't about to miss an opportunity to impress the parents, and George soon stopped listening to him. His father had often told him that his own years at the Academy had been the happiest of his death, but George had always found this hard to believe. For as long as he could remember he had been looking forward to the night when he would receive his Certificate. Then, at long last, he would be able to go out to work. His excitement had been growing ever since he had first met the Careers Officer ten years before. This was when he had decided what job he was going to take.

Of course, at the time it had been a difficult decision. With some children it was easy. They knew exactly what they were going to do from their first day at the Academy. The Celeste family,

6

for example, had a naval tradition which went back for centuries and Marie had always known that she would be going to sea. Then there was Albert Crypt. He had been destined for the church ever since he had been a shapeless lump of protoplasm on his mother's knee.

Unfortunately the Ghastly family had no such tradition. George's father maintained this was because the Ghastlies had always moved with the times. He himself worked in multi-storey car parks while George's mother had gone into tower blocks. Mr Ghastly often said that he hoped one of his descendants would be the very first ghost on the Moon.

When George had mentioned this to the Careers Officer, Mr Coffin hadn't been enthusiastic. As he had pointed out, George might well find himself stuck out there in space with nobody to haunt. Besides, he had added, nobody was quite sure what effect the lack of gravity might have on ghosts. George hadn't been at all upset to hear this. He had only suggested the Moon to please his father.

'Do you have any other ideas, George?' Mr Coffin had asked.

'Not really, sir,' George had answered. 'I was hoping you might be able to help me.'

The problem was that George had never been one of the best pupils at the Academy. He wasn't a dunce by any means. He wasn't like poor Teresa

Tomb who would have to spend her entire death creaking doors or tapping at windows. All the same, George wasn't clever enough simply to float into any job he wanted. Screaming was the subject he had done best in, and this was what he would have to do once he left the Academy. Even so, it wasn't going to be easy.

'Two hundred years ago there would have been no problem,' Mr Coffin had sighed. 'Those were the nights, when there just weren't enough of us ghosts to go around. That was before the housing shortage, of course. So many of the houses nowadays just aren't suitable for haunting, what with all this double glazing and central heating. I ask you, how can any self-respecting ghost be expected to put a decent chill in the air? To make it worse, those humans will insist on knocking down the good old houses. You'd be amazed how many of the old ghosts have to retire long before they start to fade away. I just don't know what things are coming to.'

'I'd heard times were difficult.'

It sometimes seemed to George that the old ghosts never talked about anything else.

'You don't know the half of it, young fellow. Take television, for example. It must be the worst thing that has ever happened to us ghosts. Those humans spend so much time watching it, they don't have a chance to develop their imagination. Would you credit it, there are thousands and thousands of them who don't believe in ghosts any more. Have you ever heard anything quite so ridiculous?'

Mr Coffin had continued like this for quite some time but in the end they had decided on a job which had satisfied both of them. George hadn't wanted a council house, and Mr Coffin hadn't had any unhaunted mansions on his books, so they had agreed George should become a traveller until something better came along. A peripatetic ghost was the way Mr Coffin described it, although George didn't really know what 'peripatetic' meant. George wouldn't have a house of his very own to haunt at first, but Mr Coffin was sure the travelling would do a lot to broaden his experience.

'Who knows?' Mr Coffin had added as George was about to leave. 'You might come across a place which suits you before I have a suitable vacancy.'

Once this had been settled, George had studied hard for his 'H' Levels and he had done well, even in difficult subjects like Alchemy and Poltergeistics. Now he was about to receive his reward. Up on the stage Mr Wraith had at last finished his speech and was calling out the names of those children who were leaving the Academy. Marie Celeste, Quentin Quasimodo, Ursula Venom. One by one the names of George's classmates were called out and one by one they went up to the stage to receive their certificates. Then, at last, the great moment arrived.

'George H. Ghastly,' Mr Wraith announced, his voice rustier than ever.

Proudly George left his place beside his parents and floated forwards, listening to the shrieks and moans of applause. Then the precious batskin certificate was in his hand and he was floating back again. George was no longer a schoolboy. He had become a ghost.

Two

'Well,' said Mrs Ghastly.

'Well, well, well,' said Mr Ghastly.

George's grandfather, Hadrian, didn't say anything. He simply pulled his toga closer about him and looked over George's shoulder. By now the Ghastly family was at home and George was reading through his certificate for the umpteenth time. So was old Grandfather Hadrian. As he kept on telling everybody, when he first became a ghost they hadn't had academies or certificates. Young ghosts had simply had to learn their jobs as they went along.

If the truth was known, old Hadrian was a little bit jealous. It really was a magnificent diploma, written on the very best quality batskin, the blood-red letters standing out boldly. *Ghost's Certificate of Haunting*, it said at the top. *This is to certify that in the Centennial Examination for the Ghost's Certificate of Haunting* GEORGE H. GHASTLY *has passed at the level indicated in the subject(s) shown below.* Underneath were all the GCHs George had passed. If there weren't quite as many of these as some other children had, the list still seemed impressive.

'Well,' Mrs Ghastly said again. 'I suppose you'll be out tonight, Horrible.'

Horrible was what the H. stood for in the middle of George's name. It was what his mother called him when she was in a good mood. When she called him George he always knew he was in for trouble.

'Of course he will, Mother,' Mr Ghastly answered for George. 'This is his big night. Why, I can remember my own first haunt as though it was only yesternight. It was . . .'

'We can all remember it,' Hadrian interrupted rudely. 'You've told us all about it so many times we haven't had a chance to forget.'

They would probably have started on one of their arguments, but George realized what was about to happen and decided to stop it.

'Do you have any special tips for me, Dad?' he asked quickly.

'I don't know about that, son.' Mr Ghastly was clearly flattered by the request. 'Mr Wraith and the other teachers must have taught you everything you need to know.'

'They told me what to do,' George agreed, 'but that's all book-learning. As you're out haunting every night I thought you might have some special advice you could give me.'

'I suppose I have at that,' Mr Ghastly began. 'I . . .'

'Oh no he hasn't,' Hadrian interrupted again. 'We don't want George picking up any bad habits before he has even started.'

This time there was no stopping the argument so Mrs Ghastly and George left the two men to it. As Mrs Ghastly often said, they had been squabbling for the last seven hundred years and they would continue squabbling until Hadrian eventually faded right away.

'It's time you were going, Horrible,' she said, giving George a hug. 'You don't want to be late for work your very first night. I'll say goodbye to your father and grandfather for you. Good haunting.'

Before George knew quite what was happening, his mother had pushed him through the wall and he was outside the house. Suddenly he felt very nervous and alone. He would have liked to float back inside again but he knew he couldn't. He was grown-up now and proper ghosts didn't go and cry on their mother's shoulders. Holding his head high, George started to float away from the house. His eyes were watering a little, but this wasn't going to stop him scaring the pants off his first victim, whoever he might turn out to be.

As George drifted along the quiet streets, he was trying to remember everything he had ever been taught about a successful haunt. He knew it was no good simply barging in anywhere. What he wanted was an old house where somebody lived alone, preferably somebody with a nervous disposition. Although the first few houses George tried already had ghosts, he refused to settle for second best. George was determined to find the very best place possible. However much he might want to start haunting, he certainly wasn't going to rush in just anywhere. He intended to find somewhere he could stay for a week or two while he tried out all the things he had been shown at the Academy.

It took time for George to find what he was looking for but at last his patience was rewarded. Although it wasn't a very big house, it stood on a street corner in its own garden and George knew at once that he'd feel at home there. Several tiles were missing from the roof, paint was flaking from the windows and doors, the chimney pot looked as though it would be blown down in the next strong wind and the garden was a jungle of weeds. Best of all was the beech hedge which had never been trimmed. It had grown so high that none of the neighbouring buildings were visible from the garden.

If he had had any fingers, George would have crossed them as he drifted silently up the path. The house was so perfect, George was convinced some other ghost must have beaten him to it.

'Hello,' George called, using the voice that only ghosts and dogs could hear. 'Is there anybody here?'

A dog started barking in one of the houses down the road but that was all. When George looked around he could see none of the little signs which usually showed a house was being haunted. It seemed as though George was in luck. The house would do very nicely until he found something better.

It was far too late to do any haunting that night. Of course, George could have woken up the people who lived there, but he knew this wouldn't be very satisfactory. It certainly wouldn't be worthy of a spirit who had graduated from the Academy of Ghosts. One of the very first things he had been taught was that atmosphere was everything. The air had to be nicely chilled, all the groundwork had to be done. This would be wasted if the victim was fast asleep.

George decided to spend the rest of the night finding his way around. Silently and invisibly he drifted through every room and into every cupboard. By the time he had finished George knew everything there was to know. He knew that a Mrs Pincer lived there with her two nippers. (Ghosts have a weird sense of humour and George found this very funny.) There was no sign of a Mr Pincer so George assumed he must have nipped off somewhere. (George thought this was even funnier than his joke about the children.)

In the morning George was still there, although neither Mrs Pincer nor the children had any idea there was a ghost in the house. George would have liked to go home and tell his parents all about it, but he decided to wait until he had carried out his very first haunt. Then he really would have a story to tell.

During the day George watched and listened. He watched Mrs Pincer give Tommy and Ellen breakfast and pack them off to school. Then one of the neighbours, a Mrs Crabbe, came in for a coffee and a chat. (While he was listening to them George made up lots of Crabbe and Pincer jokes but as none of them were funny except to ghosts I shan't bore you with them.) All day long, except for when she went out to do some shopping, George was never very far from Mrs Pincer's shoulder. The more he saw of her, the more convinced he became that she would be the perfect victim. She was even afraid of spiders so goodness knows what she would do when she saw a real, dead ghost.

George had decided to concentrate on Mrs Pincer alone as it was his first haunt. Despite his impatience to get started, he made himself wait until both children were safely tucked up in bed. Then, when Mrs Pincer had finished tidying up and was sitting comfortably in front of the television, George began his preparations. If Mr Wraith had been there to watch, he would have been proud. Everything George did could have come from one of the Academy's textbooks. He chilled the living-room to exactly the right temperature. He provided all the little background noises, the creaks, the tappings and the squeakings. Most important of all, George didn't rush himself. Eager though he was, he managed to contain himself until everything was just right.

Mrs Pincer behaved just the same way as the victims described in *Hints for Haunts*. At first she was unaware of anything unusual happening. She was watching a programme on television and she didn't have any attention to spare for what George was doing.

In any case, George wasn't really doing a lot apart from lowering the temperature. He hadn't ever seen television before, and he was as interested as Mrs Pincer. What made the programme especially fascinating was that it was something called a horror film. The hero reminded him very much of one of Grandfather Hadrian's friends from the old nights. Not that George had ever met him, mind you. He was far too young for that, but he had heard all of his grandfather's stories more than once.

When the programme had finished, however, Mrs Pincer suddenly realized how cold it was in the room. She shivered and pulled her cardigan closer about her. This was the signal for George to start in earnest and the more strange noises George made, the more nervous Mrs Pincer became. When she switched off the television and peered anxiously at the door which George had been creaking for the last few seconds, he knew the moment had come.

George was so excited he almost started breathing as he floated across the room to be behind her chair. Mrs Pincer was really frightened by now. She must have sensed the sudden chill as George went past her because she swung round to stare at where George was hovering. As George was still invisible, she couldn't see anything, but she was beginning to realize there was somebody or something in the room with her. Smiling to himself, George waited until she had turned away again before he made himself visible. Then George stretched out one trembling, ghostly hand and tapped Mrs Pincer on the shoulder.

It was as though the poor woman had received an electric shock. Mrs Pincer did all the things which people do when they are tapped on the shoulder by a ghost. Her hair stood on end. Her false teeth chattered. Her glasses slipped down her nose. Her knees started knocking together like castanets. Slowly, unwillingly, dreading what she knew she would see, Mrs Pincer swung her head round. And as she turned to face him, George did what he could do best and screamed.

'*Whaaaaaaaaaaaaaaaaaa!*'

It was a magnificent scream. It was even better than the scream which had won George third place in the Academy of Ghosts Terrifying Noises competition. It was the most bloodcurdling, heart-stopping scream George had ever produced. Or so George thought.

For one long second Mrs Pincer wasn't quite sure what to do. Her eyes bulged at the terrible sight. She raised one shaking hand to point weakly at the ghastly apparition. Her mouth fell open. And then . . .

And then Mrs Pincer began to laugh. George had never, ever witnessed anything quite like it. She chuckled, she chortled, she guffawed. She laughed and laughed until the tears were rolling down her cheeks. She laughed so much she slid off her chair and rolled on her back on the floor, kicking her legs in the air. She laughed so hard she was afraid her sides would split.

As for poor George, he just didn't know what was happening. He had expected Mrs Pincer to scream with terror, or faint, or drop dead with heart failure. The last thing he had anticipated was for Mrs Pincer to treat him as though he was the funniest thing since jokes had been invented. As he hastily became invisible, George was already muttering to himself.

'I must have overdone it,' he said. 'I've frightened her out of her skull. The poor old dear is as nutty as a fruitcake.'

He would have continued, but at that moment the door of the room burst open and the two children came rushing in to see what was the matter. Their mother had made so much noise she had woken them both up. They could hardly believe their eyes when they saw her rolling around on the carpet, roaring with laughter.

'What on earth is the matter, Mum?' Tommy asked.

He was the eldest.

'I . . . I . . . I . . .'

Mrs Pincer was still laughing far too much to be able to answer. All she could do was wave a limp hand in the direction of where George had been floating.

'Was it something you saw on television?' Ellen asked.

Mrs Pincer shook her head, great tears of laughter rolling down her cheeks. 'Don't worry, children,' she gasped. 'I'm all right.'

She was as well, apart from the odd hiccup of laughter. She even managed to push herself up off the floor.

'You weren't all right a minute ago,' Ellen pointed out. 'Otherwise you wouldn't have been rolling on the floor. What were you laughing at, Mummy? It must have been something ever so funny.'

'Oh, it most certainly was.'

Mrs Pincer started to laugh again at the memory. 'But what was it?'

'It . . . it . . . it was a . . . a . . .'

'A what?'

'A . . . a ghost.'

Mrs Pincer was doubled over with laughter again but she was laughing on her own.

'A ghost!' the children said together.

Instinctively they moved closer to one another, their faces white. George only had to look at them to realize that they didn't find ghosts at all amusing. He suddenly realized he might not have wasted his evening after all. He could forget about the madwoman, Mrs Pincer. George would go and haunt somebody who showed a bit of respect to a hard-working ghost.

'Tommy,' Ellen said, pulling her blankets up to her chin. 'Are you cold?'

'It is a bit chilly now you mention it,' Tommy agreed. 'Go and see if the window is open.'

'You go.' Ellen had no intention of leaving her bed. 'You're nearer.'

George smiled to himself as Tommy reluctantly climbed out of bed. He waited until the boy was halfway to the window, then made a loud creaking noise in the corner of the bedroom where the shadows were deepest. Tommy dived back into bed and shot under the blankets, shivering like a badly set blancmange.

'What was that?' he asked nervously.

'I d-d-don't know,' Ellen answered. Her teeth had started to chatter. 'P-p-perhaps it was the cat.'

'Mum put the cat outside. I saw her.'

'P-p-perhaps it was a mouse then.'

The two children lay still in their beds and listened. The more frightened the children became, the happier George was. This was what haunting was all about. It was just as much fun as the teachers at the Academy had promised it would be. He made a tapping noise over by the door.

'D-d-do mice kn-kn-knock at doors?'

'Of course they don't.'

'I th-think it's a gh-gh-ghost.'

'Don't be silly, Ellen.' Tommy's voice was beginning to shake now. 'You're imagining things.'

George kept himself invisible and made a horrible moaning noise. It sounded as though somebody was having all their teeth taken out without an injection.

Ellen gave a little scream and vanished under the blankets while Tommy sat bolt upright in his bed. By now even his ears were trembling. After a few seconds, when there were no more mysterious noises, Ellen poked her head out again. It was the moment George had been waiting for. He was floating between the children's beds when he

23

made himself visible. While Tommy and Ellen were still staring at the ghostly apparition, he went into action.

'*Whaaaaaaaaaaaaaaaaaa*,' he went.

The whole room seemed to shake, and for a few wonderful seconds it was the very best time of George's death. Every hair on the children's heads stood up on end. Their hands went up over their mouths. Their faces turned as white as the sheets on their beds.

'*Whaaaaaaaaaaaaaaaaaa*,' George went again.

And then . . . and then the children started to laugh. No circus clown ever had a better audience than Tommy and Ellen. They shrieked and they hooted with laughter. Tommy laughed so much he rolled out of bed and Ellen had to clutch her stomach because it ached.

'They are mad,' George muttered angrily to himself, hastily making himself invisible again. 'The whole family is weak in the head. They must be as daft as dodos.'

But even as he was saying this to himself, a part of George knew that it wasn't true. Mrs Pincer might have been a mistake, but now the children had reacted the same way, George couldn't fool himself any longer.

'Oh dear,' Ellen gasped in between chuckles. 'Have you ever seen or heard anything like it, Tommy. I've laughed so much I hurt all over.'

'Same here,' Tommy agreed from the floor. 'Mum was right. That ghost really is funny. I hope he comes back every night.'

As both children began to laugh again, George turned slowly and sadly away, two great ghost tears running down his cheeks. Now he knew the awful truth. He was a failure. He was the first ghost in the whole of history who made people laugh instead of terrifying them out of their wits. As he floated miserably away, George wondered what would become of him. What use was a ghost who couldn't haunt?

Three

'The shame of it,' Mr Ghastly moaned. 'To think it should happen to a son of mine.'

He was so upset that he had left his head on the table while he floated up and down the room.

'And what about the Academy?' Mr Wraith groaned. 'What are the other parents going to think when they hear about it? This has never happened to one of my pupils before.'

His head was on the sideboard, and he was floating up and down beside Mr Ghastly.

'My poor little Horrible,' sobbed Mrs Ghastly, cuddling George in her arms. 'What a terrible experience it must have been for you.'

George was feeling more miserable than ever, and being cuddled by his mother wasn't doing a great deal to help. Mrs Ghastly specialized in horrible smells when she was out haunting, and whenever she was upset she smelled even worse than usual. At the moment she was filling the room with the odour of rotten eggs. George, who was closest to her, wasn't enjoying it one little bit.

His homecoming had been even worse than he

had expected. The whole family had been waiting to hear how he had managed, together with some of the neighbours, and no sooner had George drifted in through the wall than Mr Wraith arrived. He was organizing a Sponsored Haunt to raise funds for the Academy, but had stayed on to hear George's news. George had never felt quite so ashamed as when he had to admit that he only made people laugh. Neither his parents nor Mr Wraith laughed, although George had a sneaking suspicion that some of the neighbours were amused. His father had told them so many times what a great ghost George was going to be, they must have found it very funny to learn he was a failure. One of them, old Gregory Ghoul, had been quite nasty before he left.

'I think this should be reported to the Ghost Council,' he sniffed. 'We can't have George bringing all the rest of us into disrepute.'

The only person who hadn't joined in the general chorus of wailing was Hadrian. He sat quietly in his rocking chair, looking more faded than ever, and listened to everything without saying anything himself. George had thought this was because Hadrian was too upset to speak, but he was wrong.

'A fat lot of help you all are,' he said suddenly. Although he was having one of his bad days, and there were whole minutes when his arms faded completely away, Hadrian's voice was surprisingly firm. 'Instead of feeling so sorry for yourselves, why don't you try to think of something to help George?'

'That's very easy for you to say, Hadrian,' Mr Ghastly snapped. 'George isn't your son. I know I was never a disappointment to you.'

'You weren't, weren't you,' Hadrian snapped back. 'Who was the young idiot who tried to haunt a shop full of tailor's dummies? Who was it who was so surprised when they didn't scream?'

Mr Ghastly's face, on the kitchen table, went a bright red, and the rest of his body stopped floating up and down.

'You're always bringing that up,' he said. 'It was a mistake anybody might have made. You said so yourself.'

'That was what I said at the time,' Hadrian agreed. 'I was only being kind because I didn't want you to be upset.'

That was enough to keep Mr Ghastly quiet. However, Mr Wraith still had more he wanted to say.

'It's no good covering up for your grandson,' he told Hadrian. 'Nothing like this has ever happened in the entire history of the Academy. There's no way we will be able to keep it quiet.'

'I don't see why not, Walter.' Hadrian was beginning to enjoy himself. 'After all, I can remember when you were a youngster yourself. There was one occasion I seem to recall when you put your head down somewhere and couldn't remember where you had left it. The rest of us spent three days searching for it before we found it at the bottom of that dustbin. We managed to keep *that* quiet.'

'I certainly never heard about that.' Mr Ghastly was clearly interested. 'What happened exactly?'

'Never mind about ancient history,' Mr Wraith said quickly, eager to change the subject. 'It's George's problems we have to worry about.'

'I'm glad you have remembered that at last.'

Old Hadrian was beginning to flicker in and out of visibility, a sure sign that he was angry. There was no saying what might have happened if George hadn't managed to pull himself free of his mother's arms, and put the question which was so important to him.

'What can anybody do for me?' he asked. 'I'm a complete failure as a ghost and that's all there is to it.'

The word failure made George start sobbing again, but he took care to stay well away from his mother. Mr Wraith vigorously nodded his head, in agreement with what George had said. He had forgotten where he had left it, and it nearly toppled off the sideboard on to the floor.

'George is absolutely right, Hadrian,' he said once his head had stopped wobbling. 'The poor boy is beyond anybody's help. Even special tuition from me probably wouldn't do him any good.'

'I'm sure it wouldn't,' Hadrian said nastily. He had stopped flickering but he was still annoyed. 'What George needs is for somebody to cast a spell on him.'

'A spell?' When Mr Ghastly laughed it sounded like metal being scraped against stone. 'What on earth will the old boy think of next? This is the twentieth century, Hadrian. All those witches and wizards you're so fond of telling us about vanished hundreds of years ago.'

'Did they now? That's where you're wrong, Mr Cleverclogs.'

Hadrian had started to flicker again.

'Are you sure, Hadrian?' Mr Wraith clearly didn't believe him either. 'The same thing happened with the witches as it did with the wizards. They grew younger and younger until they simply disappeared.'

'That's what happened to most of them,' Hadrian agreed, 'but not to the mightiest wizard of them all. And, I might add, the Welsh Wizard happens to be a close personal friend of mine. At least, he was when I last saw him three hundred and fifty years ago.'

'The Welsh Wizard?' Mr Ghastly's head was shaking on the table. 'I've never heard of him.'

'Well, that was what he liked to call himself.' Hadrian was sounding rather defensive now.

'Everybody else called him the Wizard Yu-u-u-ck.'

'I know who Hadrian means,' Mrs Ghastly said. 'He was the wizard whose spells and potions always tasted so foul. None of the humans would buy them and he went out of business.'

'He sounds as though he'll be a fat lot of help,' Mr Ghastly whispered to Mr Wraith, but he had forgotten how close his head was to where Hadrian was sitting. Mr Wraith made it worse by laughing.

'All right,' Hadrian said angrily. 'If that's how you all feel I shan't say another word.'

And he didn't, not for the next quarter of an hour anyway. He probably wouldn't have spoken even then if George hadn't begged him. As George kept pointing out, he had been listening even if the others hadn't, and he was the one Hadrian was trying to help. Mrs Ghastly helped as well. She said she would bring in some brimstone tea and newt's eye pasties for everybody while Hadrian continued his story.

Hadrian grumbled a bit at first but he soon allowed himself to be persuaded. As he nibbled a pasty, he explained that the Wizard Yu-u-u-ck hadn't been the fool everybody thought him. Although his potions tasted revolting, they had actually been better than those made by the other wizards. He simple refused to put in any artificial flavouring because he said this only made the spells weaker. All the other wizards sold strawberry and banana and smoky bacon flavoured spells, so people stopped going to Yu–u–u–ck any more.

'He was the clever one, though,' Hadrian continued. 'Once he didn't have to waste his time making up love potions and muck like that he could work on really important magic. That's why he is the only one left. He managed to find a spell which stopped him from growing any younger.'

'But what does he do with himself?' Despite himself, Mr Ghastly had become interested in Hadrian's story. 'Surely there's not much call for wizards nowadays.'

'You'd be surprised. I know the people in Wales still go to him – I heard he did quite a lot of work for the Welsh rugby team. Then there are his experiments. He was fiddling with the weather when we last met. He doesn't like hot weather very much and he was trying to arrange things so the summers were as cold as the winters.'

Mr Ghastly would have liked to ask some more questions about the last of the wizards but George was ahead of him.

'How will the Wizard Yu–u–u–ck be able to help me?' he asked. 'Does he make spells for ghosts?'

'There's a first time for everything,' Hadrian answered. 'He'll soon whip up a potion to put your little problem right.'

'You mean he'll make me frightening?'

'I don't see why not. He should be glad to help once he learns you're my grandson.'

For the first time that night George felt really cheerful. It seemed as though he wouldn't have to be a failure all his death after all.

Four

The first thing Mrs Ghastly wanted to do was bustle off into the kitchen and begin preparing some food for George on the long journey which lay ahead of him. However, Mr Wraith stopped her. He explained that there were plenty of cobweb sandwiches left over from Speech Day which were becoming beautifully stale. Although he had been saving them for himself as a special treat, he wanted George to have them. This was just to show that an ex-pupil wasn't forgotten by the Academy. After he had collected them, George thanked his family and Mr Wraith for all their help and said goodbye to them. He had to put up with another big hug from his mother, but he was soon on his way.

The journey itself took a little longer than it should have done, mainly because George took the wrong train at Crewe. All the same, before he knew it George was standing at the foot of Snowdon, looking up to where the wizard had his home. Although Yu–u–u–ck had cast a spell on his cave which made it invisible to humans unless they knew the secret, George could see at once where it was. Humans could walk right past and not know it was there, but to George it was as clear as night.

George knew the wizard must be at home. Every few seconds the mouth of the cave would be lit up by a great purplish flash which would be followed by a thunder-like rumble from inside. Yu–u–u–ck was evidently inside practising his magic, and George suddenly felt very nervous. Hadrian had given him one word of warning before he had left home – George must remember to be very polite, because the wizard was famous for his terrible temper. George was thinking of this temper now as he slowly started up the mountainside.

The closer George came to the cave, the more nervous he became and, as he floated up, he nibbled at the last of the cobweb sandwiches – he always felt like eating something when he was frightened. By now George had realized what the sound of thunder really was. It was the wizard's voice as he chanted out a spell. George made sure he didn't listen to any of the words, just in case the spell should have some effect on him.

At the cave entrance George stopped and took a cautious peek inside. The wizard was standing at the back of the cave in front of a huge cauldron which was being heated over a small fire. Great clouds of purple steam were billowing from the pot, and whatever it was which bubbled inside was giving off a strange glow. The wizard was still chanting his spell and all George could see of him was his back. This was frightening enough. The Wizard Yu–u–u–ck was so tall that the tip of his pointed hat almost scraped the high cave ceiling. He was wearing a long cloak which fell right to the ground, and was covered with strange symbols and designs. There were more of these on his hat.

The most frightening thing of all was the huge white cat which sat on the wizard's shoulder. Although the wizard appeared to have no idea that George was there, the cat had already seen him. It kept one eye closed but the other, which was a bright yellow, was staring directly at George. After the cat had examined him for a few seconds, it turned its head and spoke into the wizard's ear.

'Hey, Yu–u–u–cky old mate,' the cat said. 'We have a visitor.'

'A visitor? At this time of the morning?'

The wizard's voice was so loud it made the very walls of the cave tremble. When he swung round, the wizard made George tremble as well. Yu–u–u–ck had a long white beard, which had been tucked into the belt of his cloak to stop it dragging on the floor. He also had a beaked nose and two fierce eyes which seemed to burn into George as the wizard looked at him. If he was surprised to see a ghost hovering there, he certainly didn't show it.

'Well?' When the wizard spoke sparks seemed to flash from his eyes. 'Don't just stand there like an idiot. What do you want?'

'P-p-p-p-pl-pl-pl – ,' George started.

No matter how hard he tried, the words just wouldn't come out. He was so frightened they seemed to stick together in his mouth.

'Come on,' the wizard thundered. 'I haven't got all day. You can speak, can't you?'

George nodded his head to show he could. Nevertheless, when he tried again, he was no more successful. The wizard was clearly becoming impatient. He was frowning menacingly by now, with his eyebrows drawn together in a great white bar across his forehead. George was certain the wizard was about to do something truly horrible to him, like turning him into a human. Fortunately, the cat spoke again before he had a chance.

'Don't be hasty, Yu–u–u–cky,' it said. 'The poor ghost can't speak because he's terrified of you.'

'Really?' Yu–u–u–ck seemed delighted by this piece of information. 'Why should anybody be frightened of a harmless old wizard like me? Well, we'll soon fix that.'

The wizard pointed a long, boney finger at the quaking George and muttered a few words under his breath. Although George didn't feel anything, something had obviously happened.

'Now, let's have no more messing around,' Yu–u–u–ck told him. 'Spit out what you have to say and then I can go back to preparing my breakfast. It will be spoiled unless I get back to it soon.'

'Please, Mr Wizard.' George found that the words came out perfectly now. 'If you would be so kind, I'd please like you to make me a spell. Thank you very much, Mr Wizard.'

George wasn't sure whether or not he had overdone it. Hadrian had warned him to be polite and he had certainly done his best. Unfortunately it didn't appear to have much effect on Yu–u–u–ck.

'Would you ever?' he said sarcastically. 'Fancy coming to a wizard for a spell.'

'Remarkable,' the cat agreed. 'Truly remarkable.'

By now George was very close to tears.

'My grandfather Hadrian told me to come to you,' he sniffed. 'He said you were the only one who could help me.'

'Hadrian?' Yu–u–u–ck bellowed. 'Did I just hear you mention Hadrian?'

George nodded his head, not sure whether he had said the wrong thing again.

'Are we talking about the same chap?' Yu–u–u–ck roared excitedly. 'An old fellow who flickers on and off like a neon light. Wears Roman clothes or some such nonsense.'

'That's right.'

George was beginning to realize that the wizard was pleased for some reason.

'And you say that he is your grandfather?'

George nodded his head again.

'Why didn't you say so before?' Yu‒u‒u‒ck came over and put an arm round George's shoulders while the cat started licking his ear. They both stopped when they realized that although they could see George, they couldn't touch him. 'Old Hadrian did me a very good turn once. One of the very best, he was. Did he have any message for me?'

'Not really,' George told him. 'Hadrian just asked me to remember him to you. He was sure you would be able to help me. He said you were the best wizard there was.'

'Hadrian is right, of course.' Yu‒u‒u‒ck was very good at accepting compliments. 'That's why I was still wizarding while all the other idiots were squawking and gurgling in their cradles. Exactly what is your problem?'

George told him. Although he felt embarrassed explaining how bad a ghost he was, both Yu‒u‒u‒ck and the cat listened attentively.

'Well I never,' said the cat when George had finished. 'I've never heard anything like that before. Have you, Yu‒u‒u‒cky old mate?'

'I do wish you wouldn't keep calling me that,' the wizard said irritably. 'It ruins my image. I have to agree, though. It is an exceedingly strange tale.'

Yu–u–u–ck leaned forward to take a closer look at George. Although his eyes looked very fierce, he was rather short-sighted.

'Yes, I can see it now,' he said. 'Now you mention it, you are rather a comical little fellow. Still, there's nothing wrong with that. From what I read in the newspapers, the world can do with a few good belly laughs.'

'But I'm a ghost,' George explained patiently. 'People should be frightened of me. They should faint with terror at the very sight of me.'

'Well, I don't know about that.' Yu–u–u–ck sounded doubtful. 'Old Hadrian was the nicest ghost I ever met, and he never frightened anybody.'

'That's just because he is so old. He keeps fading away in the middle of a haunt.'

'He was the same when he was younger,' the wizard told George. 'Hadrian was always damned good company, if you'll excuse my language. He was always the death and soul of any party.'

'I want to be able to frighten humans.' George wasn't nearly so frightened of Yu–u–u–ck now and he was becoming more confident. 'That's what ghosts are for.'

The wizard hummed and hawed for a few

seconds but at last he agreed to help George. He refused to alter George's appearance – he said he liked him too much the way he was – but he promised to put a spell on his voice which would more than compensate.

'You'll make me really terrifying?' George asked eagerly.

'You needn't worry about that, young fellow,' Yu–u–u–ck assured him. 'When you open your mouth to scream you're going to be the most terrifying ghost the world has ever known.'

If he hadn't been so excited, George might have noticed the sudden twinkle in the wizard's eyes. Hadrian had forgotten to warn him that Yu–u–u–ck was very fond of practical jokes.

When George saw what was going into the spell, he could understand how the wizard had earned his name. There was an abcessed alligator's tooth, the eyeball of a cross-eyed canary, the nail-clippings of a sloth, two hairs from a warthog's nose and several other ingredients which looked so horrible that George was glad he didn't know what they were. Yu–u–u–ck mixed them all up together in his second best cauldron, chanting a magic chant while the cat helped him with the choruses. As he worked on it, the mixture became a treacly, black goo which smelled even worse than it looked.

'It's coming along nicely,' Yu–u–u–ck an-

nounced after a few minutes. 'Hand me a glass, will you?'

'I can't,' George answered. 'Ghosts can't pick things up.'

'It's all right,' Yu–u–u–ck told him. 'All the stuff in the cave has been ghost-proofed. It won't pass through your hand or anything like that.'

When George experimented, he found he could lift the glass as easily as he could all the things in the Ghastly home. He took it over and stood by the wizard as he stirred the foul-looking potion, muttering a few more verses of the chant. By now a pale, greenish steam was rising from the cauldron and it gave off a stench which made George feel quite ill. The smell didn't appear to worry the wizard at all. He gave the concoction a last stir and then stood back, rubbing his hands together in satisfaction.

'I think that should do it,' he said cheerfully, sniffing appreciatively. 'With a good dollop of this inside you, young fellow my lad, you're going to be the most terrifying thing since I don't know what.'

He took the glass and ladled a generous measure of the obnoxious goo into it. Although the potion was much more liquid than it had been, it was still thick and black and bubbled in the glass like molten sludge. Yu–u–u–ck held out the glass and George reluctantly accepted it. Now the time

44

had come to drink it, he wasn't quite so sure he wanted to be frightening.

'Do I really have to drink this?' George asked nervously, holding the glass well away from him.

'What do you think you're supposed to do with it?' Yu–u–u–ck roared. 'Take a bath in it?'

'Perhaps he was going to dab it behind his ears and use it as perfume,' the cat suggested.

The cat laughed so much at his own joke that he nearly fell off the wizard's shoulder. However, Yu–u–u–ck completely ignored him.

'Of course you drink it, you protoplasmic prat,' he bellowed. 'Every last drop of it. Come on, knock it back. I've wasted more than enough time on you already.'

George tried very hard to be brave, swallowing the entire glassful in one mighty gulp. Even the smell hadn't prepared him for how awful the potion actually tasted. For a moment the taste quite took his breath away. When George could speak again there was only one thing he wanted to say.

'*Yuuuuuuuuuuuuuck!*' he bellowed in a voice almost as loud as the wizard's.

'Tasty, was it?' asked the cat with a broad grin.

George hardly heard him because the strangest things were happening to him. One instant he felt so hot he was sure steam must be coming out of his ears, nose and mouth. The next he was so cold he could have grown icicles on his nose. Fortunately the sensation only lasted for a few seconds. Then he was back to normal apart from the taste of something vile and rotten at the back of his throat.

'Is that it?' he asked shakily.

'It is,' Y–u–u–ck answered. 'Unless, of course, you fancy another dose.'

'No thank you,' George was quick to say. 'One glass was quite enough.'

'In that case, be off with you,' Yu–u–u–ck told him. 'I have important work to do and you have people to haunt. Don't forget to give my regards to old Hadrian when you see him.'

George only stayed long enough to promise he would and thank the wizard for his help. Then he was out of the cave and floating down the mountainside as fast as he could go. Speedy though he was, George could hear the wizard back at work long before he reached the foot of the mountain. At least, this was what George thought he could hear. He wasn't to know that the sound of thunder was Yu–u–u–ck laughing at the joke he had just played.

Five

George could hardly wait to see whether or not
the spell had worked. There was no question of
returning home. It was almost dark when George
reached the foot of the mountain, and he decided
to try his first haunt in one of the nearby farm-
houses. The first house he tried was already
occupied by a rather bad-tempered ghost who
sent George packing, but the next one he chose
seemed perfect. The farmer, a Mr Williams, was
on his own as his wife and children were in
Llandudno on holiday, and he appeared to be a
very good test for the wizard's magic. Mr Williams
didn't look the type to believe in ghosts. He was
a short, roly-poly man with a red face, who was
kept far too busy about the farm to have time for
flights of fancy. George felt he was just the kind
of challenge he needed. Yu–u–u–ck had promised him he would be the most terrifying ghost
ever, and George knew he would need to be to put
a real scare into Mr Williams.

Despite his impatience, George was unable to

start the haunt until nearly nine o'clock. Mr Williams was so busy, he never stopped moving for more than a few seconds at a time. If he wasn't feeding the chickens, he was milking the cows, or tinkering with the engine of his tractor, or some such odd job. It wasn't until Mr Williams decided to take a bath that George had his chance.

Of course, George would normally never have considered carrying out a haunt in a bathroom. It was very difficult satisfactorily to chill a small room filled with steam. Besides, ghosts were usually the things furthest from the minds of people taking a bath, who were usually wondering how they could wash the awkward bit in the middle of their backs, or why they had a hair growing on their big toe. However, George was too excited to wait any longer. As far as he was concerned, it was the bathroom or nowhere.

Although George had no way of knowing this, the bathroom was very important to Mr Williams. He wasn't a rich lowland farmer who could simply sit back and watch the crops grow. He and his family had to struggle to make a living, and until a few weeks before there had been no bathroom in the farmhouse. When anybody had wanted to take a bath, they had had to use an old tin tub in front of the fire. This had been better than nothing but it was sometimes embarrassing when visitors arrived unexpectedly. Then Mr Williams had heard from a neighbour that the local council was offering grants for home improvements. There was only one improvement he wanted – to have the finest bathroom in the whole of north Wales.

Since the bathroom had been built, the night-time bath had become one of the highlights of Mr Williams's day. Once the day's work was done, on went the hot tap and off went his clothes. All the same, Mr Williams never rushed himself. He didn't go into the bath merely to make himself clean. He went there to make up for all the other days in his life when he hadn't been able to have a bath. With him went his pipe, his newspaper, his radio and, when Mrs Williams wasn't at home, a thermos flask full of coffee. The bath was where he intended to stay until it was bedtime, even if his skin became so wrinkled he looked like a large, pink prune.

When George came drifting through the steam, Mr Williams looked a very strange sight. Most people look a bit funny when they are in the bath but he definitely looked a lot funnier than most. Because he didn't like his hair getting wet, he was wearing his eldest daughter's frilly blue swimming cap on his head. And, because he had never lived in a house with a bath before, his big toe was stuck up the hot tap. Nobody had ever told him when he was a boy that this was a silly thing to do. All Mr Williams knew, or cared, was that this saved him from leaning over to turn on the tap when he needed more hot water. He simply unplugged his toe from the tap and the water came gushing out.

There Mr Williams lay, as happy as could be. He was puffing away at his pipe, which stuck up out of his mouth like a submarine's periscope, his loofah was in one hand and a cup of coffee was in the other. He didn't have a care in the world, not even when George first made himself visible beside the bath. Mr Williams wasn't frightened at all. Although Mr Williams knew George must be a ghost – after all, he could see right through him – he didn't look at all like the frightening creatures he had read about in books. This ghost had quite a pleasant face, the kind of face which made Mr Williams want to laugh or smile. Then everything suddenly changed. The ghost opened his mouth.

'Whaaaaaaaaaaaaaaaaaaaah!'

No sound quite like it had been heard since the last of the dinosaurs left the earth. It was a monstrous, spine chilling roar which made Mr Williams's blood turn to ice. It was a roar which carried far beyond the farmhouse. Bats flew squeaking from every church belfry for miles around. Sheep bleated piteously as they scurried hither and thither on the hillsides, not knowing in which direction safety lay. Children in bed pulled the blankets over their heads and screamed for parents who were just as frightened themselves.

As for poor Mr Williams, his only thought was escape. He wanted to put as much distance as possible between himself and the dreadful apparition which had scared him out of his wits. He didn't spare a thought for decency. He was out of the bath and running. Out of the bathroom, out of the house and across the fields, gibbering with terror as he ran.

And this wasn't the end of it. Mr Williams in his turn struck terror into the hearts of people who lived nearby, a wild, naked figure who dripped water as he ran, wearing a blue frilly bathing hat on his head and brandishing a loofah in his hand. Several of those who telephoned the police in their panic didn't believe he was human, jabbering about the great lump of metal the monster had where his right foot should have been. They weren't to know that Mr Williams had jumped out of the bath so fast that he hadn't had time to remove his big toe from the tap. Or that poor Mr Williams would refuse to enter a bathroom for the rest of his days. The mere mention of the word was enough to turn him pale and start him trembling.

However, it might have made Mr Williams feel a little better to know that he wasn't the only one to be scared out of his wits. Floating in the opposite direction, travelling as fast as panic and protoplasm power would allow, was George. He had reached the outskirts of Liverpool before he finally realized he was fleeing from himself.

'This just isn't good enough, George,' George told himself sternly. 'Why, you're behaving like some stupid human. I'm ashamed of you.'

It was all very well saying this but it didn't do a great deal to stop George trembling. Although it was more than an hour since he had dashed from the farmhouse, George was quaking so much he was unable to hold his shape. When he tried to materialize, the best he could manage was a large, luminous blob.

'It's bound to be better once I start to become used to it,' he decided. 'The Wizard Yu–u–u–ck told me I would be the most frightening ghost ever. I simply wasn't prepared for how frightening I would be.'

The thought made him feel a little better. It also made him remember old Ferdinand Faust. After his near scrape with the exorcist, he had refused to take the rest his fellow spirits had advised. He had gone back to work straight away to make sure he hadn't lost his nerve.

'That's what I must do,' George told himself determinedly. 'I mustn't be put off by one bad haunt. It isn't too late for me to go and scare the pants off a few more humans.'

With his new power, George knew he no longer had to bother about picking and choosing his victims. Anybody who met him was soon going to believe in ghosts, whether or not they had before. From where he was resting he could see

the lights of a tower block rising into the sky, and he didn't bother to look any further. Although he was still a little bit apprehensive, George kept telling himself he would be prepared this time. Even so, for the very first occasion in his death, George almost wished he was human. Then he would be able to stuff his ears full of cotton wool.

A quarter of an hour later the entire tower block was in an uproar. Lights were blazing in every window and all the residents were crowded on the landings, nervously asking one another what had happened. What Mr Williams had heard had been a mere squeak compared with George's latest effort. The horrific sound had been heard over the length and breadth of Liverpool. It had been so loud it had rocked the building, and nobody could agree what had happened. Some said it was Concorde, some said it was an explosion, others said it was an earthquake. There was even one old lady who said the Loch Ness monster must have come to the Mersey on holiday but nobody paid her any attention. She hadn't been quite right in the head for years.

The only people who might have explained what had really happened were in no position to speak to anybody. They were the young couple whose flat George had visited. They had been so terrified they had both jumped straight out of the window, forgetting that their flat was on the fifteenth floor. They would have been killed if the window cleaners who were working on the building hadn't left their cradle right outside the window. This was where the couple were now, swaying dangerously high above the ground. Although both of them were screaming for help at the tops of their voices, the other residents of the building were making so much noise they weren't discovered until morning.

And what of George? Sad to say, experience hadn't made him any less frightened. He had gone out of the window too, even more terrified than he had been at Mr Williams's farmhouse. As he had forgotten to make himself invisible, many people saw him travelling overhead and the next morning one local newspaper had the headline UFO SPOTTED OVER LIVERPOOL. This was of no concern to George. By the time his panic had subsided and he sank exhausted to the ground, Liverpool was many miles behind him. No matter how hard he tried, George was unable to hold back his tears, and he spent the night hidden in a hollow tree, sobbing quietly to himself. It seemed he had no future as a ghost at all.

Six

'I'll probably end up a nervous wreck,' George said out loud. 'I'll end up jumping at my own shadow.'

Morning had found George as miserable as ever and the old ghost joke didn't do anything to cheer him up. What good was a ghost who couldn't haunt? This was the question he kept asking himself and, unfortunately, the answer was only too clear. He was no good at all.

It had been bad enough when humans had laughed at his efforts, but now it was even worse. George knew he could never go back to his family to explain what had happened. He could just see their faces when he said that now he frightened himself. He could imagine how all the other ghosts would laugh behind his back when they heard the news. There was only one thing left for him to do. He would do what he had thought of earlier, hide himself away where he would have no contact with humans or other ghosts. At the thought of such a lonely death, more tears welled into George's eyes.

However, it wasn't long before he changed his mind. As soon as he left the protection of the hollow tree, George realized where he was. The previous night he had been too upset to pay attention to his surroundings, but now he could see the snow-capped peak of Snowdon only a few short miles away. At once George knew what he must do. He would go back to Yu–u–u–ck and ask him to remove the spell. Although he would still have to hide away, he would hide as himself, not the monster the wizard had turned him into. George would far rather be funny than scare himself to life every time he opened his mouth.

'He is coming,' Yu–u–u–ck chortled, peeping out of the cave. 'I told you he would.'

'What else could the poor soul do after what you did to him?' the cat asked. 'There are times, Yu–u–u–cky old mate, when I don't think you are very nice to know.'

'Call me Yu–u–u–cky old mate once more and I'll show you just how unpleasant I can be,' the wizard snapped. 'I'll turn you into a haggis and send you to Scotland for Burns' Night.'

'You wouldn't.'

The cat didn't sound too sure of himself.

'Just try me, that's all. In any case, you're the one who isn't being fair. I was doing that young fellow a favour.'

'You were?'

The cat clearly didn't believe him.

'Of course I was,' Y–u–u–ck told him. 'From what I have seen of the world nowadays, people need more things to cheer them up. There is enough to frighten them already. I hope young George will realize that now.'

As George floated towards the cave entrance, he didn't know he was the subject of discussion or that the wizard had been expecting him. In fact, he was dreading what Yu–u–u–ck might say when he saw he had returned, and the nearer George came to the cave, the slower he floated. All the same, he had to get there sometime. When he peered in the entrance he could see the wizard sitting at a table, leafing through a book which was filled with strange writing. On his shoulder as usual was the cat and he was the first to spot George. At least, this was what George thought.

'You have a visitor, Yu–u–u . . . , Wizard Yu–u–u–ck.'

The cat had remembered the warning just in time.

'A visitor?' Yu–u–u–ck boomed, pretending to be surprised. 'At this time of the morning?'

'It looks like that young ghost again,' the cat told him. 'Perhaps he has come to thank you for casting such a good spell.'

Yu–u–u–ck closed his book with a bang and looked up.

'Well?' he roared. 'Don't just stand there. Come in and tell me why you are disturbing me again.'

George stepped nervously forward, keeping a

safe distance between himself and the wizard. Yu–u–u–ck frightened him almost as much as his spell had done the previous night.

'P-p-p-pl-pl-pl – ,' George began.

'Great galloping gremlins,' Yu–u–u–ck shouted. 'Don't let's have that again.' He snapped his fingers. 'Now, start from the beginning.'

'Please, Wizard Yu–u–u–ck, it's about your spell.'

The wizard's magic had once more miraculously untied George's tongue.

'I told you so,' the cat interrupted him. 'He's come to thank you.'

'Let him finish. Is that why you have come?'

Miserably George shook his head.

'You haven't?' The wizard's eyebrows drew together and sparks seemed to flash from his eyes. 'You haven't come to complain about my magic, have you?'

'Oh no, Wizard Yu–u–u–ck,' George answered quickly. 'It was a marvellous spell and it worked beautifully. The only trouble was it worked a little bit too well.'

'Too well? What on earth are you babbling about? How can a spell work too well?'

To George's eyes, the wizard still looked furious. He didn't realize Yu–u–u–ck was trying very hard not to laugh.

'I didn't simply frighten humans,' George explained. 'I frightened myself as well.'

And then the whole sad story came pouring out. George told it all while Yu–u–u–ck and the cat listened. By the time George had finished he was very close to tears.

'What exactly do you want me to do?' Yu–u–u–ck asked.

Although George was too upset to notice, the wizard's voice was much softer than it had been before.

'I'd like you to remove the spell, please,' George said.

'You mean you want to be the way you were before, when everybody laughed at you?'

'Well . . .' George hesitated. 'I don't suppose you could give me another spell which isn't quite so strong?'

This was something which had occurred to George on his way up the mountain. He thought it was quite a good idea until he saw both Yu–u–u–ck and the cat shaking their heads.

'There are no half measures here, my little ghostly friend,' the cat told him. 'It's all or nothing.'

'I am afraid he's right,' Yu–u–u–ck agreed. 'I don't dilute my spells for anybody. Either you are terrifying or people laugh at you. Which is it to be?'

This was an easy choice and Yu–u–u–ck went to work at once. The ingredients were different and the goo was bright green but it smelled as awful as the wizard's previous potion. Yu–u–u–ck scooped up a generous glassful and held it out to George.

'Here you are, young fellow,' he said. 'Drink it up.'

'All of it?' George inquired unhappily.

Yu–u–u–ck nodded.

'In one gulp?'

The wizard nodded again and George sighed as he accepted the glass. Down went the sticky muck in one huge swallow, and it tasted even worse than the first potion.

'*Yuuuuuuuuuuuck!*' George bellowed.

'And cheers to you too,' said the cat, smiling broadly all over its furry face.

This time the after effects of the spell were different. At first George felt as though he was growing larger and larger, being pumped up like some gigantic balloon. For a few seconds he was afraid he would fill the entire cave and push out into the mountain but just as George became convinced he must surely explode, he began to shrink again. He shrank and shrank and shrank. Now George was afraid he might vanish completely, but suddenly he was back to normal. All he had left was an unpleasant taste in his mouth.

'That's it then, I suppose,' George said disconsolately.

'You are back to your original self, if that is what you mean,' Yu–u–u–ck told him.

'In that case, thank you very much for all your trouble, Wizard Yu–u–u–ck. I promise you I shan't be bothering you again.'

Before Y–u–u–ck had a chance to reply, George had turned away and drifted towards the cave entrance. The wizard opened his mouth to call him back, then decided he couldn't think of anything to say and closed it again. Although he turned his head, the cat refused to look him in the eye. There was an uncomfortable silence until they had both watched George out of sight. Even from behind George looked sad and unhappy.

'Do you want to know something, O great and mighty Yu–u–u–ck,' the cat said at last. 'You have made a right veritable shambles of that. The poor little fellow didn't appreciate your lesson at all. I think you are beginning to lose your touch.'

For once Yu–u–u–ck wasn't upset by what the cat had said.

'It wasn't one of my best efforts, was it?' he said thoughtfully.

'It most certainly wasn't, Yu–u–u–cky old fruit. Hadn't you better do something to put matters right?'

'I had indeed,' Yu–u–u–ck agreed.

Purposefully the wizard strode to the back of the cave where he began to prepare a new spell. His potions might taste horrible but Yu–u–u–ck hated to have a dissatisfied customer.

Seven

George didn't have the slightest idea where he was
or how he had arrived there. It was almost as
though he had been travelling in his sleep, because the last thing he could remember was
standing at the bottom of Snowdon. Besides, it
had been daylight then and now it was dark.
Although George knew the idea was a silly one,
it was almost as though the whole day had been
magicked away without him knowing anything
about it. Snowdon was nowhere to be seen, and
instead of being in the Welsh countryside, he was
on the outskirts of a large town. George had no
idea which large town it was. It could be Liverpool or Luton or London for all he knew.

However, there was one thing George could be
positive about and that was the name of the
owner of the large house he was looking at. He
was floating beside some ornate, wrought iron
gates and a metal plaque had been attached to
one of the gateposts. MR MERRYFELLOW, it

read. ALL VISITORS WELCOME. PLEASE RING THE BELL.

'Mr Merryfellow,' George said to himself. 'That's an unusual name.'

As George was still feeling exceedingly miserable he was trying to cheer himself up by talking to himself. The trouble was that no matter how hard he tried, he couldn't think of anything amusing to say. He just wasn't in the mood. Nevertheless, the plaque did give George an idea which he thought was entirely his own. He had no way of knowing that the Wizard Yu–u–u–ck had been at work in his cave on Snowdon.

'If he really is a merry fellow,' George continued, still speaking to himself, 'and he really does welcome all visitors, I might as well pop in and see him. I ought to test Yu–u–u–ck's new spell and make sure it's working properly. If it is, it should give this Mr Merryfellow something to be merry about.'

Despite his attempts at a joke, the young ghost didn't feel at all merry as he floated through the gates and started up the drive. He had to travel quite some distance before he had a proper view of the house, and when he could see it George temporarily forgot all about his tears. Without a doubt it was one of the strangest buildings he had ever seen in his death. The house was absolutely enormous. What was more, it looked as though it had been put together from a child's building kit by lots of different people, all of them with their eyes closed. There were towers and gables and minarets and stained-glass windows and steeples and verandahs and domes, all of them jumbled together in a bewildering hodge-podge which George found quite delightful. He wasn't to know that the people of the town thought differently. They contemptuously referred to the house as 'Merryfellow's Folly'.

'It's lovely!' George exclaimed, so excited that he spoke out loud. 'And there doesn't seem to be any other ghost in residence. Just imagine what I'd be able to do here if only I was a proper ghost.'

George was sniffing back the tears again as he set off across the lawn but it didn't even occur to him to turn back. Yu–u–u–ck's spell saw to that.

Mr Merryfellow was a small, round man without a great deal of hair. He was so shortsighted he would have worn his glasses in bed if they hadn't rubbed the skin off the bridge of his nose when he turned over. He looked even smaller and rounder than he actually was when he was curled up in the middle of the giant four-poster bed, although the nightcap he wore to keep his head warm prevented George from seeing that the only hair he had left grew in tufts behind his ears. The nightcap matched Mr Merryfellow's red striped nightshirt. A lot of people would have considered this old-fashioned, but Mr Merryfellow was old-fashioned, and he couldn't care less what other people thought about him. He liked to feel comfortable and he certainly wasn't when he wore pyjamas. The elastic in the trousers always seemed to cut into his tummy.

There were so many rooms in the house, so many corridors and staircases, George had been a little bit worried about finding his way around. However, as it turned out, this was no problem at all. Mr Merryfellow had no wife to complain to him so when he slept, he snored. First he snorted the air back up his nostrils, drawing it down into his lungs, then bubbled it out through his mouth, sounding a bit like a bad-tempered hippopotamus having a mud bath. It was a magnificent snore, loud enough to rattle the window panes in their frames, and George had no difficulty in finding his way to the correct bedroom.

For a moment or two George simply hovered beside the bed, more than a little sad because he knew this was likely to be his very last haunt. There didn't seem to be a great deal of point in making elaborate preparations. All George intended to do was make sure he had returned to normal, and no longer terrified himself every time he opened his mouth; then he would find somewhere quiet he could hide himself away. There was nothing else he could do. If he allowed making humans laugh to become a habit, he would bring the whole of ghostdom into disrepute.

Mr Merryfellow's favourite hobby was eating and he had been dreaming of treacle puddings when the noise awoke him, a horrible, bloodcurdling sound which made his toenails curl. At first he couldn't see anything. It was dark in his bedroom and he wasn't wearing his glasses so all he could distinguish was a shadowy figure standing beside his bed. With trembling hands he switched on the light and fumbled his spectacles on to his nose, terrified of what he might see. However, his terror didn't last long. As soon as he could see the ghost – and he knew it must be a ghost because he could see right through it – he was no longer frightened. It was such a comical figure, with a face rather like a wizened clown, that Mr Merryfellow began to laugh. He laughed easily at the best of times, but now Mr Merryfellow laughed as he had seldom laughed before, great guffaws which seemed to come all the way from his toes and misted up his glasses. He hadn't seen anything quite so funny since his Great Aunt Emilia had sat on a bumblebee and done an impromptu war-dance around the living-room, spilling hot tea into the vicar's lap.

As for George, he wasn't quite sure whether he was pleased or disappointed. On the one hand, he was definitely pleased to discover that he had returned to normal, that he no longer frightened himself when he haunted a human. On the other, it made him very sad to think he would never be able to return to his family or see any of his friends again. The shame of having to admit that he made people laugh still was more than he could face.

Slowly, dispiritedly, George began to drift away, off to find some place where he could hide, somewhere he would have to meet neither fellow ghosts nor humans. He would become the very first hermit ghost.

'Hey. Wait a minute. Where are you off to?'

There had suddenly been something about the expression on the ghost's face which had made Mr Merryfellow stop laughing. He was a kindly man and it always upset him to see anybody unhappy, even a ghost. As for George, he hadn't really intended to stop. If he hadn't felt so lonely, and if Mr Merryfellow's voice hadn't sounded so friendly, he would never have turned round.

'I have to be going now,' George explained. 'I won't bother you any more.'

'You don't have to go, you know.' The ghost seemed to be so miserable, Mr Merryfellow wanted to cheer him up. 'You don't frighten me at all.'

'Exactly.' Despite himself, George could feel tears of self-pity welling into his eyes. 'That proves it. I can't be much of a ghost if I don't frighten you.'

George turned away again but Mr Merryfellow jumped out of bed and rushed across the room to

stand in front of the bedroom door. He looked a bizarre figure with his white, hairless legs sticking out beneath the nightshirt and the bobble of his nightcap dangling in his left eye.

'Hold hard there a minute, young fellow,' he said firmly. 'I won't have people leaving my house unless they're cheerful. Do you have anywhere to go?'

'Where could I go?' George was still feeling sorry for himself. 'A ghost who makes people laugh isn't any good to anybody.'

'I don't know about that,' Mr Merryfellow told him. 'There are far too many frightening things in the world today. We could all do with more to make us laugh.'

'But not ghosts,' George objected. 'Ghosts are supposed to haunt people and scare them out of their wits. That's the very first thing I learned at school.'

'Piffle and poppycock. You learn lots of things at school which aren't true. Besides, you can't imagine what a pleasant surprise it is to meet a ghost who makes you laugh. I tell you what. Why don't you stay here with me? I live here all on my own so there's plenty of room.'

For a moment George could hardly believe his ears.

'Do you really mean it?' he asked.

'Of course I do. I wouldn't have suggested the idea otherwise.'

'It's really very generous of you.'

'Balderdash.' Although Mr Merryfellow tried to sound gruff, he found he had a lump in his throat. 'You'd be doing me a favour. You'd be surprised how lonely I am here sometimes. Will you stay here with me?'

George's mind was already made up. He had liked Mr Merryfellow ever since he had first seen him asleep in bed. There was something about his face which reminded George of his grandfather, old Hadrian.

'Yes,' said George. 'Yes, please. I'd love to live here with you.'

'Excellent,' Mr Merryfellow told him, blushing with pleasure. 'Splendid. Let's shake hands on it, then.'

Meanwhile, several hundred miles away in a cave on the slopes of Snowdon, both Yu−u−u−ck and the cat were hunched over the wizard's crystal ball.

'Stupid dolt,' Yu−u−u−ck growled. 'Doesn't the imbecile know that you can't shake hands with a ghost?'

'I think it's rather sweet,' said the cat, dabbing at its eye with one paw. 'I do so enjoy a happy ending.'

'What makes you think we've finished?' the wizard asked. 'It's no use doing things by halves. Now, where did I put my happy family spells?'

As the wizard started to leaf through the thick, parchment pages of his spell book, the cat began to purr quietly to itself.

George settled in surprisingly quickly. He liked the house and, more important, he and Mr Merryfellow had hit it off together right from the start. Within the first couple of nights George knew he was going to be very happy in his new home. But there was one final thing he had to do. To begin with George thought of sneaking back one night when all his family was out at work. He could gather up his few belongings, leave a note to say he was perfectly all right, and that would be an end to it. Then George thought how upset his mother would be. He owed it to her to try and explain, no matter how embarrassing an experience this might prove to be. When the problem was put to him, Mr Merryfellow was in complete agreement.

'Families are important, George,' he said. 'I know it will be unpleasant for you but it's something you have to face.'

Although George didn't know much about maps, Mr Merryfellow did, and it didn't take him long to sort out the way to the Ghastly residence. George left late one night, after Mr Merryfellow had gone to bed, and the nearer he came to his parents' home the more nervous he felt. At first, though, it wasn't too bad. Mrs Ghastly was alone when George drifted in, preparing one of her toad's liver stews, and she was too pleased to see her son to bother with any awkward questions.

However, it wasn't very long before Mr Ghastly and Hadrian arrived, arguing as usual. Worse still, they brought Mr Wraith with them. Mrs Ghastly's stews were famous and the headmaster of the Academy usually managed some excuse for floating in when she was preparing one. This was when the questions started and George's answers seemed to have exactly the effect he had feared.

'My poor little Horrible,' sobbed Mrs Ghastly, enveloping George with the odour of decomposing fish-heads. 'Whatever are you going to do?'

'The shame of it,' moaned Mr Ghastly. 'To think this should happen to a son of mine.'

'Don't you ever think of anybody except yourself,' snapped Hadrian, flickering angrily like sheet lightning at sea.

George edged cautiously away from his mother, feeling utterly miserable. Then, to his surprise, Mr Wraith came to his defence.

'I can't see any need for all this fuss,' he said.

For a moment there was a stunned silence.

'What did you say?' demanded Mr Ghastly, so agitated he was passing his head from hand to hand.

'I can't see why everybody is so upset,' Mr Wraith told him, floating up and down the room with his hands clasped behind his back in his best headmaster's fashion. 'On the contrary, I think you should all feel proud of what George has done.'

'Proud?' Mr Ghastly snorted the single word so loudly that his head slipped from his hand, ending up face down in the armchair. His next words were muffled. 'Of George? That's absolutely ridiculous. Ghosts are supposed to terrify humans, not set up house with them.'

'Why don't you try listening for a change? You might learn something.' Hadrian was clearly intrigued by what Mr Wraith had said and had temporarily stopped flickering. 'Do carry on, Walter. I want to hear what you have to say even if my idiot son doesn't.'

'Well, Hadrian,' Mr Wraith began. 'As you know, last night I attended the Grand Gathering of Ghosts, Ghouls and Apparitions and . . .'

Like all teachers, Mr Wraith was in love with the sound of his own voice, and he took much longer than was necessary to explain. It seemed that the leaders of the Ghost Council had become very worried about the future of ghosts, a worry which went far beyond the housing shortage mentioned by Mr Coffin, the Careers Officer. The GG of GG and A had discussed the whole relationship between ghosts and humans. Now that many of the old human superstitions were fading or had died away completely, ghost unemployment was at such a high level that drastic

measures were called for, and a special committee had reported to the Gathering. Their suggestion was a complete break with tradition.

Mr Wraith would obviously have continued for some time longer, but Hadrian had had enough. He had started flickering again, and he interrupted Mr Wraith in mid-sentence.

'Great galloping gremlins, Walter,' he snorted, 'get to the point, and don't be so long-winded.'

Mr Wraith was clearly upset, but what he had to say was far too important for him to stop now.

'It's quite simple, really,' he said rather huffily. 'We agreed that some ghosts should try to make friends with human beings, find out whether it's possible to live side by side.'

For a moment there was absolute silence in the room, a silence which was broken by Mr Ghastly.

'Make friends?' he said in amazement. 'With humans?'

'Exactly,' Mr Wraith agreed.

'But that's what I'm doing.' George was unable to contain his excitement any longer. 'Mr Merryfellow and I are going to be friends.'

'Precisely,' said Mr Wraith. 'You, George, will be the very first of a new kind of ghost. I don't think it's too much to say that the whole future of us ghosts may depend on now successful you are.'

Suddenly the overpowering odour of sweaty socks filled the room. Although George knew what was about to happen, he was too slow to escape.

'My darling little Horrible,' Mrs Ghastly said, cuddling George close to her. 'I'm so proud of you.'

'That's an even better ending,' said the cat, dabbing at its eyes with both front paws and nearly losing its balance.

The wizard simply pushed his crystal ball away and muttered something about getting back to work as Wales was playing England at Cardiff Arms Park the following Saturday. However, the two of them had been together too long for the cat to be deceived. He had noticed the hint of moisture in the wizard's eyes and he was purring contentedly to himself as he settled more comfortably on his master's shoulder.

'Now,' Yu–u–u–ck was saying. 'I think we'll put a non-stick spell on the English players' hands this year. That should do the trick.'

Neither he nor the cat referred to George again but this didn't mean that they forgot him. Even if you are a wizard, as old as time itself, it isn't every day you meet a ghost who makes you want to laugh.

BEAVER TITLES FOR YOUNGER READERS

If you're an eager Beaver reader, perhaps you ought to try some more of our exciting titles. They are available in bookshops or they can be ordered directly from us. Just complete the form below and enclose the right amount of money and the books will be sent to you at home.

☐	MR BROWSER AND THE MINI-METEORITES	Philip Curtis	£1.50
☐	THE GREAT ICE-CREAM CRIME	Hazel Townson	£1.25
☐	MIDNIGHT ADVENTURE	Raymond Briggs	£1.25
☐	NICHOLAS AT LARGE	Goscinny and Sempé	95p
☐	EMIL GETS INTO MISCHIEF	Astrid Lindgren	£1.25
☐	BOGWOPPIT	Ursula Moray Williams	£1.75
☐	THE FOLK OF THE FARAWAY TREE	Enid Blyton	£1.75

If you would like to order books, please send this form, and the money due to:

ARROW BOOKS, BOOKSERVICE BY POST, PO BOX 29, DOUGLAS, ISLE OF MAN, BRITISH ISLES.

Please enclose a cheque or postal order made out to Arrow Books Ltd for the amount due including 30p per book for postage and packing both for orders within the UK and for overseas orders.

NAME ....

ADDRESS ....

....

PLEASE PRINT CLEARLY